This Orchard
book belongs to

_____

_____

_____

For Romily

J.M.

For Rory (who has NO problems sleeping),

with love from Auntie Lindsey x

L.G.

ORCHARD BOOKS

338 Euston Road, London NW1 3BH

Orchard Books Australia

Level 17/207 Kent Street, Sydney, NSW 2000

First published in 2009 by Orchard Books

First paperback publication in 2010

ISBN 978 1 01616 124 0

Text © James Mayhew 2009

Illustrations © Lindsey Gardiner 2009

1 3 5 7 9 10 8 6 4 2

Printed in China

Orchard Books is a division of Hachette Children's Books, an Hachette UK company.

www.hachette.co.uk

When DRAGONS are DREAMING

James Mayhew ✳ Lindsey Gardiner

ORCHARD BOOKS

When the night comes
and the stars fill the sky,
when dragons are dreaming
the fairies fly by.

They dance in the moonlight
and skip through the trees.

They swing on the branches

and play on the leaves.

But one little dragon,
curled up in his nest,

just can't get to sleep,

though he's trying his best.

He watches the fairies

playing a game

and decides he is going
to do just the same!

"Look out!" shout the
fairies, flying away.
"Wait!" shouts the dragon.
"I just want to play!"

Crash go the branches

and smash go the trees

and crunch goes the dragon,

all covered in leaves.

"You're too big and lumpy!"
the fairies all say.
"You should be home sleeping.
You can't come and play!"

But one little fairy,
called Lily the Blue,

gets caught in a web,

now what will she do?

Here comes a hero
to rescue the fairy.

Dragons don't think
that spiders are scary.

He quickly flies over
and lifts Lily clear . . . .

... she then gently whispers
into his ear –
"Dragons aren't really
so bad I suppose."

And she flies down
and gives him
a kiss on the nose.

Then they play in the branches

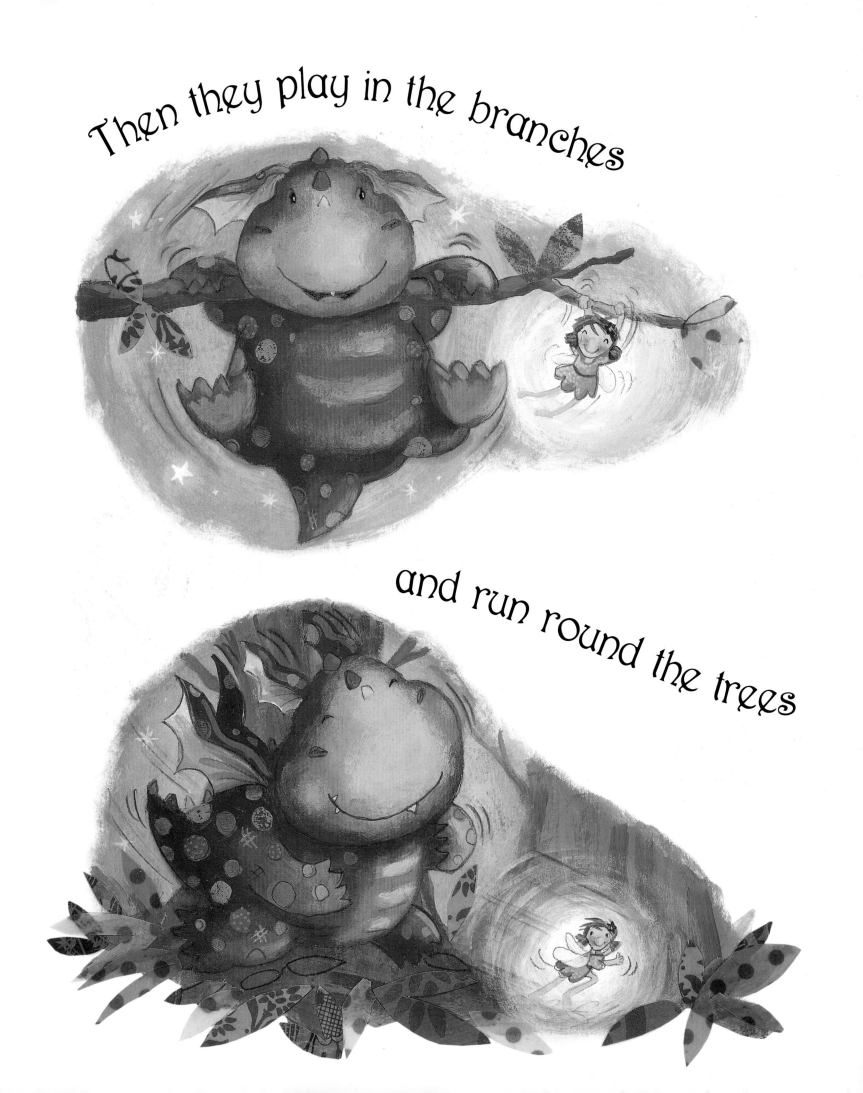

and run round the trees

and fly past the stars
on the gentle night breeze.

Tired little dragon,
our young sleepyhead,

says good night to his friend

and flies home to bed.

He cuddles his mummy,
while up in the sky,
when dragons are dreaming
the fairies fly by . . .